SPACE ADVENTURE

by the author of Noah's Rocket
TONY FRAIS

TO
CHARLOTTE

Illustrations by Rosalind Wilson

keep reading

Published in 2006 by Anthony Frais,
9 Sandhill Oval, LEEDS LS17 8EB
UNITED KINGDOM
e-mail: afrais@tiscali.co.uk

ISBN   978 09548068 11

Introduction

Stanley the Spider made his first appearance in Tony Frais' first book Noah's Rocket. A modern day Noah is instructed to build a giant space rocket in order to escape the coming flood. Along with his family, he is also instructed to take a male and female of every creature on Earth into the rocket and go in to orbit around the Earth until it was safe to return.

To find out if the flood had gone, Noah had decided that the best creature to go down to Earth would be a spider called Stanley who would attach his web silk to the rocket, spin down to Earth and pick up an object to take back to the rocket to show the flood had gone.

Wearing a protective red woolly space suit that had been knitted for him by Noahs wife, Stanley set off on his mission.

When the rocket eventually returned to Earth, all the animals were led out to return to their homes all over the world. Stanley came out of the rocket still wearing his red woolly space suit and was expected to go back to his home in the Rainforest.

However . . .

CHAPTER 1

After his adventures in space, Stanley was happy to have all eight legs back on firm ground. Standing outside the rocket, he was soon joined by the lady spider who was feeling very cold and told Stanley that she was going home to the hot Rainforest where she and Stanley had come from.

But Stanley was not feeling cold at all. He was still wearing his red woolly space suit and felt very snug and warm.

"I think I will stay here for a while," he told the lady spider. "I quite like it around here."

Stanley decided to secretly follow Noah and his wife Ethel as they made their way back home.

After a while, Noah and Ethel arrived back at their house. Stanley hid behind a hedge and waited until they had gone inside.

He slipped unnoticed into Noah's back garden.

Stanley decided that it seemed a good place to call home. Suddenly, he began to feel very hungry.

"I need to catch some lunch," thought Stanley, "and there is only one way to do it."

So Stanley climbed up the stalk of the nearest flower and started to spin his web.

It wasn't very long before lunch arrived. A large juicy fly!

At first, Stanley was content in Noah's back garden but as the days passed, he began to feel a little bored. Life in Noah's garden was not as exciting and interesting as it was in the Rainforest and not as exciting as his trip into space.

Stanley decided to go and surprise Noah. Perhaps there might be a chance of another exciting adventure with him!

CHAPTER 2

Now it just so happened that at the same time Stanley was planning on the surprise visit, Noah was watching the news on the television. He got very excited when it was announced that a special rocket had been sent into space to discover signs of life on distant planets. On its way into deep space, the rocket had sent back pictures of two small planets that were very close to one another and were showing signs of movement over the surface. The scientists who were watching these pictures were thrilled that the mysterious movements could be some sort of life!

Unfortunately, the two planets were far too small for an astronaut to land on.

"Now we will never know the secret of these mysterious planets," said the chief scientist.

Noah thought it was a great shame about that. Suddenly, he thought of an idea. Stanley would be the perfect astronaut. He would be small enough to land on the two planets. But Noah thought that his brave little friend would be somewhere in the Rainforest, thrown away his red woolly space suit and was once again spinning his web and catching flies.

He was quite wrong about that because Stanley had decided to let Noah know that he was nearer than he thought.

Noah heard some very familiar tapping on his front window. "It can't be, could it?" said Noah. He went over to the window and to his surprise and delight, it was Stanley.

"Ethel," shouted Noah, "it's Stanley – he's here at the window."

"Better let him in then," shouted Ethel.

Noah opened the window and let Stanley in. "So, still wearing your red woolly space suit," he said. "I was wondering how you were getting on. All this time I was thinking that you would be back home in the Rainforest and I suppose you've been in my back garden all along!

Stanley, you are not going to believe this, but I think you could be back in space soon!"

Stanley got very excited on hearing this.

Noah did not waste much time in picking up the telephone and calling Mission Control.

"I would like to talk to the chief scientist," said Noah. The chief scientist came on the telephone.

"I heard on the news that your rocket has discovered some unexplained movements on two planets that are too small for an astronaut to land on," said Noah. "I've got the perfect answer to your problem and he's with me now in my living room!"

The chief scientist was very interested to hear this and asked Noah just who it was in his living room. "It's a spider called Stanley," explained Noah. "He is a very experienced space traveller and small enough to land on and explore these two planets. Shall I bring him over to you?" The chief scientist asked if Noah could bring Stanley over to Mission Control as soon as possible. "I'll come over right away!" replied Noah.

Noah put the telephone down. "Stanley, it's back into space for you!"

Stanley was excited, Noah was very excited, and Ethel thought it was all wonderful. "Our little Stanley is going to be very famous!" she said.

CHAPTER 3

Noah and Stanley set off for the Rocket Centre. They walked into the Mission Control building.

"Hello, my name is Noah and I have come with my friend Stanley to see the chief scientist."

The lady at the desk could only see Noah.

"And where is this other gentleman?" she asked.

"He's here beside me," replied Noah.

"Well I can't see anybody," she said.

Noah lifted Stanley up onto the desk.

"There you are, this is Stanley." The lady jumped when she first saw Stanley, but Stanley gave her his big toothy smile.

"What a cute little spider," she said. "I've never seen a red woolly spider before – I'll let the chief scientist know you're here."

Soon the chief scientist came to greet Noah and Stanley.

"Hello there, pleased to meet you. Please come with me to my office."

Noah and Stanley followed the scientist into his office.

"So, this is the spider with space travel experience is it?"

"It is," replied Noah.

"Does Stanley know what is expected of him?" asked the scientist.

"I have told him that his mission will be to fly to these two mysterious planets, land on both of them and try and find out what is causing all these unusual movements."

"Exactly," said the scientist.

"Stanley has got what it takes. He is ready for the mission and he's already got his space suit on! I am sure the mission to find out about all these mysterious movements on those tiny planets will be a great success!" said Noah.

Noah succeeded in convincing the chief scientist that Stanley would be perfect for the mission.

"I'm sure it will be a great achievement," said the scientist. "Not only that but, because we now need only a very small rocket to send Stanley to the planets, it will be small enough for him to land safely. Well, I think that's all for today. Stanley, please report back here in two days time and be ready for blast off."

Noah thanked the scientist. "Come on Stanley, let's get you back home."

Two days later, Noah and a tearful Ethel waved goodbye to Stanley as he made his way to Mission Control for his space adventure.

CHAPTER 4

Stanley arrived at Mission Control ready for blast off. Before being taken to the rocket, he was greeted by the chief scientist who gave him some last minute instructions.

"Remember Stanley, your mission is to land your rocket on both planets, and report what you find to Mission Control. You will find these planets just behind Mars."

Stanley understood everything that was being asked of him. After receiving his instructions, he was shown into a room filled with good luck cards and even a few strange gifts which people thought might be useful to take on the trip including two very large rubber bands and an old teapot. Stanley could not think why anyone would want to send him these very odd things but something made him decide to take them on the mission.

The time had now come for him to board the rocket. The chief scientist took Stanley to the launch pad and wished him good luck on his mission. Stanley climbed aboard the rocket, closed the door behind him and took his seat in the cockpit. A few moments later, he heard the chief scientist's voice over the radio. "Prepare for blast off. Ten, Nine, Eight, Seven, Six, Five, fire rocket engines, Four, Three, Two, One, BLAST OFF."

The little rocket shook all over as the powerful engines lifted it off the launch pad on its way into space. Stanley looked back and saw the Earth getting smaller and smaller behind him. Soon he was in the deep, deep blue of outer space and heading for the mysterious planets. Stanley waved at the Moon as his rocket went past. Next to come was Mars. Stanley steered the rocket beyond Mars and then he saw the two planets that were very close to one another and directed the rocket towards them.

After a short while, Stanley was in position to land on the first planet. He set the controls and prepared for landing.

Stanley wondered about what he was going to find as the rocket gently touched down on the surface.

CHAPTER 5

Stanley opened the door of the rocket and put his feet down onto the firm ground. The first thing that he noticed was that the surface was green with grass. He hadn't been exploring for long when he came upon the sight of two little grapes lying on their backs in the sun.

Stanley was very surprised to see grapes on this distant planet. He went over to them.

"Hello!" he said. "My name is Stanley and I have come from the Planet Earth."

"Hello Stanley," said one of the grapes. "Welcome to Planet Fruton!"

"Thank you," said Stanley. "Are you the only fruit on Fruton?"

"No we are not," replied the other grape. "We come from the City of Fruitville which is just over that hill. That's where all the other fruits live."

"Thank you," said Stanley, "I'll make my way over there and pay a visit."

Stanley said goodbye to the two grapes and made his way over the hill to the City of Fruitville. "A city where everyone living there is fruit – sounds impossible," thought Stanley. Soon he came to a sign that read: *'Welcome to Fruitville. Population 2,000 and growing.'*

Walking past the sign, Stanley began to see what looked like a large town. As he walked nearer to the town he could see lots of different types of fruit going about their business.

Stanley noticed that there was one building much bigger than all the rest. He decided to make for this building. As he got to the front steps, he saw the words 'FRUITVILLE TOWN HALL' above the front door.

Stanley knocked on the door. The door opened and a plum appeared.

"Can I help you?" asked the plum.

"Yes, my name is Stanley and I have come here from Planet Earth to explore this and the other nearby planet."

"You are talking about our neighbouring planet Vegeton. We really don't have anything to do with the inhabitants of Vegeton you know," replied the plum.

"Why is that?" asked Stanley.

"Because Planet Vegeton is populated only by lowly vegetables – some of them live underground you know and most are of a very dull colour, not like us on Fruton. We are fresh and colourful and live above the

ground – some of our citizens even live in trees you know," replied plum. "Anyway, enough about those lowly folk on Vegeton. How would you like to have a guided tour of Fruitville?"

Stanley told the plum that he would be delighted to accept.

"Good, I'll go and ask the Mayor of Fruitville and the rest of the senior Town Hall staff to come and meet you."

The plum went back inside the Town Hall. Stanley thought all of this was very strange – one planet inhabited by fruit and the other by vegetables.

After a short while the Mayor appeared with other senior members of the town's committee. Stanley noticed that all of them were plums.

"Welcome to Fruton and to our fine City of Fruitville," said the Mayor.

"Delighted to be here," said Stanley, "I see that you are all plums – not a banana or orange in sight!"

"That's because plums get all the best jobs in Fruitville," replied the Mayor.

"As Mayor of this city, I have decided that I will be the one to show you the sights of Fruitville. Just follow me."

Stanley said thank you and goodbye to the other plums and followed the Mayor to begin the tour of Fruitville.

CHAPTER 6

Stanley and Mayor Plum made their way through the streets of Fruitville. Stanley noticed the open air swimming pool where lots of apples were bobbing around in the water. "I didn't know apples could float," said Stanley.

"That's because apples have quite a bit of air inside them!" replied the Mayor.

It was a very busy town, with pineapples, apricots, and the odd cherry rushing around. All the fruit seemed to be in quite a hurry. As Stanley and Mayor

Plum reached the corner of the street, a bunch of bananas flew round the corner at such a speed they bumped into Mayor Plum and knocked him over. Stanley helped to pick up Mayor Plum from the ground. "Are you all right?" asked Stanley.

"We're terribly sorry about this," said one of the bananas. "Perhaps you should go to the hospital for a check up." Mayor Plum thought that was a good idea. So he and Stanley walked to Fruitville Hospital.

"Fruitville Hospital is very good at treating bruised fruit," Mayor Plum told Stanley.

Soon they arrived at the hospital where they were greeted by Doctor Apricot.

"Welcome Mayor Plum," he said. "What's happened to you then?"

"I was knocked down in the street by a bunch of bananas," explained Mayor Plum.

"Well now, lie down on this bed and I will examine you. Hmm, looks like a bit of bruising on your back. I'll just rub some ointment in and you'll be just fine."

"Thank you Doctor Apricot, I'm beginning to feel much better now!"

Mayor Plum got up from the bed. "Come on Stanley, let's continue your tour of Fruitville."

As they were leaving the hospital, an ambulance pulled up at the entrance. Nurse Lemon opened the door and brought out an orange looking in very bad shape. Mayor Plum walked over and asked the orange what had happened.

"I was just having a quiet walk in the country when I was attacked by wild strawberries."

"Oh dear," said Mayor Plum.
"Well I'm sure you'll be well
looked after. Good luck!

We have a problem with those
wild strawberries Stanley."

Suddenly there was a loud roar
in the sky. Stanley looked up to
see a rocket flying overhead.

"See what I mean," said the
Mayor. "It's those wild
strawberries flying around in their
rocket."

The Mayor explained that many
years ago, the wild strawberries
had mysteriously found a small
rocket out in the countryside and
kept flying around in it for a bit of
fun. "We really need to do
something about those

strawberries; they are becoming quite a nuisance."

Stanley wondered how it was possible to have another rocket landing on Fruton. Had Fruton been visited by someone else before?

"Now Stanley, I am going to take you to see Planet Fruton's finest school."

Once again, Stanley followed Mayor Plum and soon they arrived at a building with a sign outside that read: 'FRUTON SCHOOL FOR GENTLEFRUIT'.

Stanley followed the Mayor into the school. They were greeted by a large pineapple.

"Hello Mayor, what brings you here today?"

"Hello Headmaster, I've brought along a very special visitor to Fruitville. This is Stanley, all the way from Planet Earth."

"Hello Stanley, welcome to the school. Here we teach, amongst other things, how to behave in a fruit bowl."

"How interesting!" replied Stanley who by now thought he had seen quite enough of the delights of Fruitville and was keen to get on with the next stage of his mission.

Mayor Plum spoke up. "How about a visit to Fruitville's old age home where fruit happily retire and live to a ripe old age?"

Stanley politely told Mayor Plum that he needed to get on with his visit to Vegeton.

"Very well Stanley, would you like to come back to the Town Hall for a fruit juice before setting off?"

"That's very kind of you. Yes, I could do with a drink," said Stanley.

Stanley and Mayor Plum arrived back at the Town Hall and they went straight to the Mayor's office.

A plum arrived with two glasses of orange juice.

"Drink it all up young Stanley, fruit juice provides vitamins and minerals that can help to keep you fit and healthy! You know we fruit are very proud of the fact that we bring good health. On top of that, most of us are very sweet to eat, not like those lowly vegetables."

The Mayor went on.

"The citizens of Fruton are far superior to those veggies on Vegeton – you'll find that out soon enough when you visit their planet."

"Have you any idea how the citizens of Fruton arrived on this planet?" asked Stanley.

"Nobody really knows the answer to that. But we are all very happy here on Fruton and I hope you will pass the message on to your friends back on Earth about the good fruit of Fruton," replied the Mayor.

"Thank you Mayor Plum, I will. Now I must get on with the rest of my mission."

Stanley said goodbye to the Mayor and made his way out of Fruitville and back to where the rocket had landed.

On his way back to the rocket, Stanley passed by the spot where the two little grapes had been lying in the sun. Stanley wanted to say goodbye but couldn't see them. Then two squeaky voices shouted, "Hello Stanley spider." Stanley turned around to where the voices were coming from and all he could see were two little crinkly brown things. "Spent too long in the sun Stanley – we're raisins now!"

Stanley laughed. "Well raisins, I'm off in my rocket to visit Vegeton."

"How exciting," said the raisins. "We've never met a vegetable before – I don't think anyone on Fruton has actually met a vegetable! Good luck Stanley!"

Stanley waved goodbye to the raisins and walked the short distance to the rocket.

Inside the rocket, Stanley thought that he should call Mission Control to tell them what he had discovered. He switched on the radio and spoke into the microphone. "Calling Mission Control, calling Mission Control, this is Stanley calling."

A voice replied, "Come in Stanley, come in Stanley, we can hear you! What have you found so far?"

"I've just completed the first part of my mission. The first planet I visited is called Fruton and the entire planet is inhabited by fruit!"

There was a long silence from Mission Control. Then a voice said, "Are you asking us to believe that you have just visited a planet inhabited by fruit – this is very very unusual!"

"You think that's unusual?" replied Stanley. "The neighbouring planet Vegeton is inhabited entirely by vegetables! Not only that, but Fruton has wild strawberries flying around in a rocket that somehow landed here many years ago!"

The scientists at Mission Control could not believe all this. They decided to keep this news a secret from the rest of the world for a while until Stanley had visited Vegeton and reported back. The scientists had to try and find out how it was possible that two planets far from Earth could be the home of fruit and vegetables. Then the scientists had another thought. "Might there be other strange planets inhabited only by chocolate sponge cakes or even different types of cheese?" But their first task was to try to understand how such a thing was possible and what of this other rocket? Where had that come from? They radioed back to Stanley and told him to proceed with his mission.

Stanley set the controls for Vegeton and prepared for blast off.

CHAPTER 7

Stanley's rocket blasted off for the very short journey to Vegeton. In fact the journey lasted only a few seconds.

On landing, Stanley climbed out of the rocket. After walking around for a few moments, he saw two peas coming towards him.

"Hello peas, I'm Stanley and I have come from Planet Earth to visit you and your neighbouring planet Fruton."

"Been to Fruton have you?" said one of the peas. "I hear the fruit are quite snobby about themselves. I've heard they don't think much of us vegetables just because we're not sweet to eat and some of us live under the ground and . . ." "Shut up Percy," said the other pea. "We're just as important to eat as those fruities. Why don't you wander over to Vegeville and meet the other veggies?"

"That's exactly what I aim to do," said Stanley.

So off he went until he came to a sign that read: 'WELCOME TO VEGEVILLE.'

Wandering further, Stanley spotted a small wooden shack that had a note pinned onto the front door which read: 'VEGEVILLE TOWN HALL.'

Stanley knocked on the door and a voice answered.

"Hello, who is knocking on the door of the Vegeville Town Hall?"

"I am Stanley the spider and I come from Planet Earth. I have visited your next door planet Fruton and now I am visiting Vegeton."

The door opened and there stood a large cauliflower.

Then a voice shouted from inside the Town Hall. "Who is it Cyril?"

The cauliflower shouted back. "It's a . . . red woolly spider called Stanley."

"Well let him in then," said the voice.

"I will do just that, Clarence," said Cyril. "Walk this way would you please, I'll take you to see the Mayor."

Stanley went into the Town Hall. On his way to meet the Mayor, Stanley noticed that all the vegetables working in the Town Hall were different, not like Fruitville where everyone in the Town Hall was a plum. Stanley was shown into the Mayor's office. Behind the desk sat a tall green cucumber.

"Welcome to Vegeton and the town of Vegeville," said the cucumber. "My name is Clarence."

"How do you do Clarence," said Stanley. " I have just come over from Fruton."

"Oh yes, Fruton," said Clarence. "We know all about those fruities."

Stanley told Clarence he was surprised that although the vegetables had never visited Fruton and that the fruit had never visited Vegeton, both of them knew about each other.

"I will tell you how Stanley," said Clarence. "A tomato by the name of Timothy was once a citizen of Vegeton, but one day he decided to go over and become a fruit on Fruton. Then he decided to come back again and become a citizen of Vegeton once again. This little tomato was never sure whether he was a fruit or a vegetable but sadly for us, he finally decided to go back and live on Fruton. When he was on Fruton, he told them all about us and when he came back to Vegeton, he told us all about Fruton. So that is how Fruton and Vegeton know about each other."

"That's very interesting," said Stanley. "But how did Timothy manage to get over to Fruton and back?"

"Ah yes, Timothy made a mysterious discovery. On a remote part of Vegeton, he found a rocket. No one knows how it got there but Timothy used it to fly over to Fruton. Then he used it to come back again and finally, he used it to go back to Fruton."

Stanley remembered about the wild strawberries on Fruton who had also found a rocket.

Stanley asked Clarence why he thought the tomato had finally decided to go back to Fruton.

"The thing is Stanley, Timothy Tomato decided he was a fruit after all.

I know those fruities are snooties and they look down on us just because some of us live underground. Not only that but apart from my secretary Carol Carrot and Sam Sweet Potato who live around the corner, we may not be as colourful and sweet to eat as they are. But I'll tell you something Stanley, it is just as important to eat us veggies! Just like the fruities, we've got lots of healthy vitamins which are very important for good health."

Stanley was very impressed with all of this. Then he had an interesting thought. "Wouldn't it be great if the veggies could go over to visit Fruton, meet up with the fruit and get to know them."

"That's not a bad idea Stanley. But how do we get over there and back?"

Stanley wasn't sure about that. Then he came up with an idea.

"What if I took some veggies over in my rocket!"

"Won't work Stanley," said Clarence. "Some veggies are quite big and you wouldn't get a lot of us in. If you saw the size of Tracy Turnip and Marvin Marrow you would know what I mean."

"Oh well," said Stanley, "perhaps I'll think of another way."

"Time for lunch Stanley," said Clarence. "I'll get some soup brought in."

Clarence called out "Waiter!" The door opened and in walked an asparagus.

"Alfred, two bowls of soup please," said Clarence. A few moments later Alfred came back with the soup.

"There you are, asparagus soup-I made it myself you know."

Stanley looked at his bowl of soup and called out, "Waiter!"

"What seems to be the problem sir?" said Alfred.

"Waiter, there's no fly in my soup!"

"I'm terribly sorry sir, I'd quite forgotten that you spiders like your flies."

"Never mind," said Stanley. Stanley and Clarence finished their soup.

"Now how about showing you around Vegeville?" said Clarence.

"Fine," said Stanley.

They came out of Vegeville Town Hall and Stanley looked upon a very peaceful scene. The citizens of Vegeville did not seem to be as busy and in such a hurry as the fruits of Fruitville. Clarence pointed out some of the citizens to Stanley. "There's Cynthia Celery walking with Bert Broccoli and over there are Chris and Cathy Corn strolling out with Baby Corn. All very peaceful you know."

Stanley agreed.

Clarence went on, "We have all the usual things here as well; schools, hospitals – much the same as Fruitville I suppose."

Stanley told Clarence he was right about that except that Fruton did have some annoying wild strawberries who kept flying around in a rocket they had found.

"Really?" said Clarence. "We don't have any problems like that on Vegeton. Still, despite those tutti fruities, I wouldn't mind visiting Fruton just to make friends, only I'm too big to get into your rocket Stanley. There's only the likes of Percy Pea and Randolph Radish who would be small enough to fit in."

Stanley agreed. But then he remembered about the strange gifts he had brought along in his rocket, and hit on a fantastic idea.

"You know Clarence, Fruton is a very short distance away, we could use the rubber bands I've brought with me to make a catapult. We just need some help from the other veggies and we could catapult you and a few other large veggies over to Fruton. I could fly over to Fruton and spin a very strong web to catch you and the others when you land. Then, perhaps with the help of some friendly fruities, we could catapult you back to Vegeton."

"Brilliant!" said Clarence, "let's do it!"

CHAPTER 8

Stanley went to his rocket and brought out one of the two rubber bands. He put one end around a celery plant and the other end around another celery plant.

"There's your catapult Clarence," said Stanley. "I'll fly over to Fruton and take the three smaller veggies; Percy Pea, Randolph Radish and Sydney Sprout with me. Then I'll weave my catching web. When I shout over that everything is alright, you can be catapulted over and Tracy Turnip and Marvin Marrow could come over as well. But first, I must weave a web on this side as well to catch you all on your return journey."

After Stanley had woven his web, the call went out to all the veggies that were going to make the trip. First to turn up were Rodney Radish, Percy Pea and Sydney Sprout.

"Good," said Stanley. "You three come with me in the rocket."

Stanley, Percy, Rodney and Sydney climbed aboard the rocket. Stanley blasted off and a few seconds later landed on

Fruton. The four climbed out of the rocket. Then Stanley began to weave his extra strength web between two apple trees. After doing that, he shouted over to Clarence. "Everything is set, you can come over now!"

Clarence was the first. A number of very strong potatoes pulled back the rubber band. Clarence took up his position in the middle of the catapult and then the potatoes let go.

There was a loud PING and Clarence was hurled across to Fruton, landing exactly in the middle of Stanley's safety web. Then it was Tracy Turnip's turn – PING – followed by Marvin

Marrow. All the veggies were now safely on Fruton.

Stanley then made another catapult with the other rubber band so that the veggies could get back.

"Let's make for the Fruitville Town Hall," said Stanley.

Stanley and the vegetables started their walk to Fruitville. Soon they came across the two raisins still in the same spot, lying in the sun.

"Hello raisins," said Stanley.

"Hello Stanley, what are those strange looking things?"

"They're vegetables from Vegeton. They are here on a friendly visit to Fruton."

"Goodness me!" said the raisin, "I've never seen a veggie before – bit funny looking aren't they? I'm not sure what Mayor Plum is going to say about all this."

"Neither am I," said Stanley. "But it's a good idea that fruities and veggies get to know one another. Well, we must be off now. See you later."

Stanley and the vegetables walked the short distance to Fruitville Town Hall. On arriving, Stanley knocked on the front door. The door was opened by one of the plums.

"Hello Stanley, you back again? How were things on . . . what is this! Who are all these strange looking things with you?"

"They are a party of visiting vegetables from Vegeton. They have come to make friends and get to know the fruit of Fruton."

"Well I never," said the plum. "I'd better get the Mayor at once!"

Mayor Plum came to front door. "What's all this then Stanley?"

Stanley explained to Mayor Plum that it would be a good idea to have a get together and sit around a table so that the fruit and veg can find out about one another.

Mayor Plum thought that this would be a good idea.

"Would you all like to step this way," he said.

Stanley and the veggies followed Mayor Plum up to his office.

CHAPTER 9

"Please take a seat at the table," said the Mayor. "If you could wait for a few minutes, I'd like to invite some of the other fruities to attend this meeting."

Mayor Plum left the office and a few minutes later returned with an apple, an orange, a banana and a cherry.

The fruit sat opposite the vegetables and it was the apple that opened the meeting.

"Let's get this right straight away; we fruities are the healthiest food. We are full of healthy vitamins and minerals.

Eating us several times a day is enough to keep everyone fit and healthy and we're much sweeter to eat than you lot."

"Just a minute," said Percy Pea. "Peas are quite sweet and so are carrots and sweet potatoes and we are also full of healthy vitamins and minerals. Eating us several times a day is just as important to keep everyone fit and healthy!"

"Well said!" said Clarence. "Not only that, but you can put all sorts of things on us like cheese on cauliflower, salad dressing on your lettuce – nobody would want to eat an orange covered in melted cheese would they!"

"Well who would want to eat an onion covered in cream?" said the cherry.

"But think of how wonderful strawberries are covered in cream."

"That reminds me Mayor Plum," said Stanley interrupting the argument. "What happened to your wild strawberry problem?"

"Oh we sorted that one out Stanley. After you left, I called out Fruton's feared Red Berries, who went out and arrested those strawberries responsible for attacking the orange and flying around in that rocket. We locked them up in Fruton prison – that's where the bad fruit go. But enough of that. It seems to me that the veggies are saying that eating enough of them is just as important for good health as we fruities and, if you think about it, we fruities wouldn't feel at home on the same plate as roast beef."

The other fruities thought about that for a minute and decided that Mayor Plum was right. All the fruities stood up and walked around the table to shake hands with the veggies. The veggies were so happy with this act of friendship and understanding that Tracy Turnip was almost in tears.

"What a wonderful meeting this has been," said Mayor Plum. "To think that I was also a snooty fruitie who looked down on the good folk of Vegeton. Now I know the veggies are just as important and healthy to eat as we are."

Stanley was so happy to hear all this. Meanwhile, orange was in a deep discussion about music with Tracy Turnip.

"How about the Fruton Symphony Orchestra coming over to give a concert in Vegeville?" he said.

"Great idea," said Tracy. "My sister Tina Turnip sings with a rock'n'roll band The Heavy Potatoes. Perhaps they could come over and play for the fruit."

Mayor Plum had overheard this and was a little worried. "How do the fruit and veg get over to one another's planet?" he wondered. Then he realised there was something he needed to ask Stanley.

"Stanley, how did you get all these veggies over to Fruton?" Stanley explained about the catapult.

"Well that solves the problem," said the Mayor.

Meanwhile, the other fruit and vegetables were busy planning visits to each other's planet. Apple told Percy Pea his idea about having two identical schools built on each planet so that fruit and vegetables could go and learn all about one another.

Stanley could see that everyone was getting along just fine and perhaps his mission was about over and it was time to return to Planet Earth.

Stanley called out, "Fruities and Veggies, thank you both for having a really happy meeting. I must get back to Planet Earth."

Both the fruities and the veggies thought Stanley was the greatest spider of all time.

"We'll all come with you to see you off," said Mayor Plum.

So Stanley, along with the fruit and veg began the walk back to the rocket.

CHAPTER 10

It was not long before the party of fruit and veg reached Stanley's rocket.

"Well Stanley," said Mayor Plum. "Thanks to you, the fruit and vegetables are going to get along just fine. Don't worry about the veggies getting back, I'll ask some pineapples to pull the catapult. Have a safe trip home."

"Thanks Mayor Plum," said Stanley.

All the fruit and veg shouted goodbye and thank you to Stanley as he boarded his rocket.

Stanley set the controls for Earth and blasted off from Fruton for the last time.

Stanley put in a call to Mission Control.

"Come in Stanley, we can hear you."

Stanley told them all about what had happened and that he had not been able to solve the mystery of how the fruit came to be on Fruton and the vegetables on Vegeton. Also, there was the question of how it was that both the fruit and vegetables had found a rocket on each of their planets.

Mission Control decided that someone on Earth might be able to explain these mysteries so they decided to make a news announcement to the world about what Stanley had discovered and asking whether anybody could offer an explanation.

Within five minutes of the announcement, Mission Control received a telephone call from a Professor Shmaltz. Professor Shmaltz provided Mission Control with the answer to the mystery of Fruton and Vegeton.

Just in case the Earth was going to be destroyed by another flood, the professor had decided that it would be a good idea to save the fruit and vegetables. He thought the best way of doing this would be to fill two rockets, one with all the fruit seeds, and the other with all the vegetable roots and seeds. His intention had been to aim the rockets at the moon so that they would land safely and, one day, astronauts could go to the moon and collect all the seeds and roots to re-plant them back on Earth. Unfortunately, Professor Shmaltz's aim was not too good. The two rockets blasted off but missed the Moon by at least a hundred miles and carried on into outer space. Professor Shmaltz told Mission Control what must have happened next. One rocket must have landed on Fruton, burst open and scattered the seeds. The other rocket must have done the same thing when it landed on Vegeton. This must have been how the fruit and veg got to grow and inhabit these far away planets!

The news was relayed to Stanley who was, by now, almost at the end of his journey back to Earth. As Stanley's rocket got very close to Earth, he looked down and could see the Rainforest far below and for the first time in a long time, Stanley felt homesick.

CHAPTER 11

Stanley's rocket finally touched down. On climbing out of the rocket, he was greeted by the chief scientist and his old friends Noah and Ethel.

"Well done Stanley," they all said.

"Fancy getting fruit and vegetables to become good friends – I suppose you will be looking for another space adventure after such a magnificent achievement," said the chief scientist.

Stanley said he wasn't quite certain about that and anyway he had noticed his home in the

Rainforest from space and thought that perhaps it was time to return to see if things were alright.

"Well if things are not all right in the Rainforest then I couldn't think of anyone better to sort it out," said the chief scientist.

Stanley asked if he could borrow the rocket for the last time so he could get home.

The chief scientist agreed.

"Ethel and I will really miss you Stanley," said Noah.

Stanley said he would miss them too, but he was sure that one day they would meet up again.

"Well, I suppose I won't need my red woolly space suit anymore, so perhaps I should take it off."

"I wouldn't do that if I were you," said Ethel. " You are very important and famous now and you will only be recognised by your red space suit."

Stanley thought about that and decided that it wouldn't do any harm to keep it on.

So Stanley said goodbye to everybody and climbed aboard the rocket.

Setting the controls for his home in the Rainforest, Stanley blasted off, happy to be going home again. He was very happy with his latest space adventure. Happy that the mystery of Fruton and Vegeton had been solved and how lucky he was that someone had given him two rubber bands to take on the trip. But as Stanley looked around the rocket as it sped its way to the Rainforest, he spotted something and realised that there was one final mystery that he could not solve.

Why did someone send him an old tea pot?

Stanley Says:

"Remember kids, eat at least 5 portions a day of fruit and veg to help keep you fit and healthy."

If you liked this book you can read about Stanley's other adventures in Noah's Rocket.

Visit Stanley's Website www.noahsrocket.com

TEACHER'S NOTES

- Stanley's Space Adventure focuses on the issue of conflict and reconciliation linking to the Citizenship/RE curriculum.

- Conflict and reconciliation is a feature relating to Attainment Target 2 in RE – Learning From Religion.

- Included are some suggestions for activities regarding fruit and veg in terms of healthy eating/environment/art-design.

- The strength of a spider's web is highlighted.

FOR KEY STAGES 1 & 2

Unit 5: Living in a Diverse World. Section 1

Pupils should be able to:

- begin to recognise and respect the similarities and differences between people in different places

FOR KEY STAGE 2

Unit 13 How do we deal with conflict? Section 1

Pupils should be able to:

- define conflict

- identify different kinds of conflict and why they arise

- understand how conflict begins and how it affects individuals and communities

CITIZENSHIP ISSUES AND ACTIVITIES

- How are we the same but different? For example, the story identifies the fact that both fruit and veg are equally nutritionally important even though they have different colours and shapes.

- If you were Stanley in this adventure – how would you sort everyone out? How would the children start dialogue and reconciliation?

- Pupils should understand and explain the need for reconciliation and dialogue in their own lives

- Role play – how would you behave if you were a fruit meeting a vegetable for the first time?

- Discuss symbols of peace e.g the dove of peace. Let pupils design their own symbol for reconciliation e.g a pear and a carrot holding hands.

- Make fruit and veg puppets etc to make a puppet show.

FOR MORE INFORMATION AND IDEAS FOR LESSON PLANNING VISIT www.dfes.gov.uk/citizenship click on 'Schemes of Work' then click on 'select a subject' then click on 'Citizenship KS1 & 2'.

HEALTHY EATING/environment/art-design

- Why is it important to eat at least 5 portions of fruit and veg a day?

- Find out where different fruit and veg grow in different places e.g. do oranges, pineapples or bananas grow in England? If not, why not?

- Did the tomato in the story make the right decision to become a fruit rather than a veg?

- Is Clarence Cucumber really a vegetable? Could he be a Fruton spy?

- Find out where your favourite fruit and veg come from.

- Visit a place that sells fruit/veg – survey what is grown locally.

- Design my favourite fruit/veg badge.

- Groups game – find others who like your favourite fruit/veg.

- Design your fruit/veg group poster.

- Design funny lunches – could fruit be eaten with veg? i.e. apple and beetroot sandwiches.

- Compose the Fruton and Vegeton anthems.

- Food tasting blindfolded (watch out for allergies)

- Have a cookery club – make own fruit and veg cookery book

FOR MORE INFORMATION VISIT
www.food.gov.uk/healthiereating then click 'nutrition' on the left hand side menu.

THE STRENGTH OF A SPIDER'S WEB

In the story, Stanley weaves his web to make it strong enough to safely catch the vegetables that are catapulted across from Vegeton to Fruton.

- Naturally occurring spider silk is widely recognised as the strongest, toughest fibre known to man.

- On a weight basis, the web of a spider is stronger than steel.

- It has been estimated that if a spider could weave a giant web with each strand being the thickness of a pencil, it would be strong enough to catch a jet passenger plane in full flight.

INTERESTING WEB FACTS.

- Not all spiders weave webs.

- Parts of the web are woven using sticky silk to catch prey. The silk is elastic enough to prevent prey from rebounding off the web.

- Webs lose their stickiness after a day. Spiders eat their own web so the protein used for making the silk is recycled.

ACTIVITY

- Considering its relative strength, can pupils suggest other uses for spider silk thread?

For example, fishermen of the Solomon Islands use spider silk to make fishing nets.